SITTI
AND THE
CATS

*A
Tale
of
Friendship*

Copyright © 1993 by Sally Bahous
Illustrations copyright © 1993 by Nancy Malick
Published by Roberts Rinehart Publishers
Post Office Box 666, Niwot, Colorado 80544
and Barbara J. Ciletti
2219 Judson St.
Longmont, CO 80501

Published in the United Kingdom, Ireland, and Europe by
Roberts Rinehart Publishers, Main Street, Schull,
West Cork, Republic of Ireland

Published in Canada by Key Porter Books,
70 The Esplanade, Toronto, Ontario
Canada M5E 1R2

Printed and bound in Hong Kong

Library of Congress Cataloging-in-Publication Data

Bahous, Sally.
    Sitti and the Cats / by Sally Bahous ; illustrated by Nancy
Malick.
        p.   cm.
    Summary: A poor old woman who lives alone in a small village has a
magical encounter with elegantly dressed talking cats, whose
generous gifts help her bring an understanding of the value of
kindness to a selfish neighbor.
    ISBN 1-879373-61-0 : $13.95
    [1. Fairy tales.   2. Folklore—Palestine.]   I. Malick, Nancy,
ill.   II. Title
PZ8.B14   Si   1990
398.21'095694—dc20
                                                    90-31080
                                                        CIP
                                                        AC

SITTI
AND THE
CATS

A
Tale
of
Friendship

by Sally Bahous
illustrated by Nancy Malick

ROBERTS RINEHART PUBLISHERS
ODYSSEY BOOKS

About
Palestinian Tales

Palestinian fairy tales appear designed to teach children as well as to entertain them. These fairy tales dwell on what is socially accepted and necessary in village life. For example, in "Sitti," the importance of careful housewifery is almost catalogued; frugality with food, cleanliness, and sharing with neighbors are almost a necessity in small villages for the survival of all. There is almost always an element of magic in Palestinian stories almost in defiance of reality. Reality is often harsh and to soften that reality, there is a "what if" element of make believe. The magic always works for good, for the betterment of some character that deserves a better life. Good characters are those who display the characteristics necessary for living in small communities; generosity, friendliness and never selfishness. Indeed, evil is often defined in these fairy tales as selfishness, and good is defined as putting the good of the community and others before self. The themes of the stories I remember from my childhood had to do with how people should behave; a person's behavior to self, to others, to community, and to the environment.

سالي

Sally

*To Katie
and
all other children
who cannot grow up
in the magic
of Palestine.*

Introduction

I grew up in a magical land called Palestine where children were the center of every village's existence. Everyone in our village of Shafa' Amer knew everyone else, so we all watched out for one another. We children were welcomed in all the houses in the village. If we fell and hurt ourselves while playing far from our own houses and our own mothers, we knew that other mothers would be there to clean our hurts and soothe our feelings and give us good things to eat. Palestine was a magical land because we knew we were safe in our walled village, safe from the fear of wild animals and strangers and hurts and hunger.

Life in Palestine was also magical because we were surrounded by stories. There were stories to explain everything about our lives. We had stories explaining why it only rained in the gray winter and why all summer long not a drop of moisture ever fell from our blue, cloudless skies. We had stories explaining why our village and the surrounding hillsides were catacombed with caves: caves under our houses to store grain; caves to shelter our donkeys and goats and sheep; caves to store water for the long, dry summers; and caves out in the hills where wild animals lived and where sometimes, like in the story of Ali Baba, thieves lived. Palestine was a wonderful place to grow up, because whenever we children grew tired of playing our important games or climbing trees or exploring one another's houses, we could always find someone's grandfather or grandmother to tell us one or several of the stories of our homeland.

That is how I first heard this story I have chosen to tell you. Since we spoke Arabic in Palestine, the names in this story may sound strange to you.

In Arabic, *Sitti* means "lady" and is sometimes used to mean "grandmother." *Im* means "the mother of," so that *Im Yusuf* means "the mother of Joseph" since *Yusuf* is "Joseph" in Arabic. *Malika* means "queen," and *Leila* means "night." Both are popular names in Arabic. Now you know enough Arabic to understand the story of *Sitti and the Cats.*

So, for one storytelling time, may you be safe and snug in my magical Palestinian village, listening to a voice as old as time tell you about life as it could be lived.

Not so long ago in a small village in northern Palestine, where I grew up, there lived a little old woman whom all the villagers called *Sitti*. She had outlived her husband and her children and so she was all alone in the world. Sitti lived in a little old house and made her living by raising a few chickens and selling the eggs they laid. In the spring and summer and autumn, she grew her own vegetables, and with the grain that she was allowed to glean from her neighbors' fields, Sitti had enough to eat. Her life was simple but satisfying.

Every morning Sitti would wake up and collect the eggs her hens had laid. Then she would deliver the eggs to her customers. When she returned to her house, she would tend her vegetable garden and begin cooking her meal. Every day Sitti would sweep and tidy her few belongings, singing as she worked around her one-room house. In the afternoons Sitti would sit in her doorway under the jasmine vine, mending the clothes that her egg customers would give her to do in exchange for a few extra piasters. With the money she earned mending clothes and selling eggs, Sitti could buy the staples she needed, such as flour and sugar and tea. Sitti did not have to buy olives and olive oil, which were so important in the villagers' diets,

To glean means to come after the harvesters and to pick up whatever produce is left in the fields or on the trees.

2

because she was allowed to glean the olive orchard. The olives she could glean after the harvesters had finished were usually good enough to pickle, and the owner of the orchard gave Sitti enough oil to use in exchange for taking care of his children one week every year when he took his wife and went to visit relatives in Damascus.

For her supper, Sitti would have cucumbers and the cheese she made from the milk that her neighbor, Ali, gave her in exchange for eggs. After her meal, Sitti would sit outside in the cool of the evening and talk with Im Yusuf, another old woman who lived next door to her.

DAMASCUS is the oldest, continually inhabited city in the world. Damascus is in Syria and has a famous "souk" or market place.

3

Unfortunately, Im Yusuf had a sharp tongue
and for that reason her son's wife would not
let her live with them. It was the custom in
Palestine, you see, for grandparents to live
with their children. Sitti felt sorry for Im
Yusuf because she would have been happier
living with her son and his family. Im Yusuf
did not have to earn her living, however,
and always had plenty to eat and wear
because her son did take care of her. So Im
Yusuf had lots of time to visit the villagers,
and she always had gossip to tell Sitti in the
evenings as they sat under the trees.

IM means "mother of."
YUSUF is the Arabic
pronunciation of "Joseph,"
so "Im Yusuf" means the
"mother of Joseph."

4

In the spring and summer and fall, Sitti's life was pleasant. All her days were much the same, and she enjoyed them. But when winter came, life was not so pleasant. In fact, life in the winter was harsh for Sitti. The garden did not produce eggplants and tomatoes and peas and cucumbers and beans. This meant that Sitti had to rely on the dried beans and peas she had managed to save during the summer. In the winter, the cold and wet weather made the hens stop laying eggs, so Sitti had no money to buy staples. And though the winter was not very cold in Palestine, it was cold for little old women. Sitti tried to keep warm by wearing many layers of clothing, and she tried to take the chill out of the house by burning the twigs and branches that were pruned from the olive orchard in the fall.

BRAZIER is an open container which stands on legs used to heat a room. It is usually made of brass and charcoal or wood is burned in it. Some braziers have lids with open ornate designs on them to allow heat to escape.

One particular winter, the weather was colder than usual, and Sitti could not get warm. After three days of heavy rain, Sitti had run out of branches and twigs for her fire. Her little house felt damp and cold, so when the sun came out in the afternoon of the fourth day, Sitti put on her boots, pulled her shawl over her head, and put a frayed pair of wool socks over her hands. She walked against the wind to the olive orchard and began to gather the twigs and sticks that had blown down in the wind of the previous days.

Sitti soon had her arms full and was just ready to turn back home when she heard a meow. She turned to look for the cat who had cried so sadly. There was no cat to be seen. But the meow came again, a long, even sadder sound.

Palestine is filled with olive orchards, some very ancient. Olive trees might die, but their trunks and roots can live for a long time and produce new growth. Palestinians use olives to pickle and eat as well as to press for olive oil which is used to flavor Arabic food. The olive tree has a gnarled trunk which is easy to climb. The tree is evergreen and has finger-shaped gray-green leaves.

Winter in Palestine is the rainy season. In the summer, no rain falls, but in winter there is rain almost every day. The earth in Palestine is catacombed with caves, and fissures which capture the rain water and hold it. Plants send out roots into this water source in the dry summer time. Northern Palestine where Shafa' Amer is located is fertile and has always grown an abundance of vegetables. There are wonderful wild flowers in this part of Palestine in the spring, such as anemones, cyclamen, tulips, and narcissus.

This time Sitti looked up into the trees, and there, not far above her head, sat the strangest kitten Sitti had ever seen. The kitten had an ordinary enough little black face and green eyes; what made her strange was that she was wearing a lavender dress and a little yellow scarf. Sitti stared and stared at the strange cat, and then, remembering her manners, she said, "Oh, pardon me for staring so at you, but I've never seen a cat dressed as you are."

"Is my dress torn or dirty?" the kitten asked.

"Oh, no," answered Sitti, forgetting in her excitement that cats can't talk.

"Please, Sitti, would you get me down out of this tree?" the kitten begged.

"Dear me," said Sitti, "I'm so old and I haven't climbed a tree in many a year, but I'll try."

So Sitti carefully put down her bundle of twigs and sticks, hoisted her skirts up and tied them around her waist, and began to climb the olive tree. Fortunately, it was an old, gnarled tree which provided many footholds, so Sitti managed to get up high enough to lift the kitten onto her shoulder and climb back down. When they were both safely on the ground, Sitti rearranged her skirts, picked up her bundle of twigs and sticks, and took a good long look at the little kitten she had rescued. Sure enough, the kitten had on a lavender dress and a yellow scarf, and she sat there looking at Sitti as she licked her paws and straightened her fur.

"Thank you, Sitti," said the kitten in a polite voice. "Would you come home with me now and have some tea and cakes?"

Now, Sitti was tired and she would have loved the luxury of tea and cakes, but she could not imagine who the kitten belonged to and was shy about going to a stranger's house.

"I'd love to, kitten," she replied, "but as you can see, my arms are full and I really need to get home and get warm."

"Oh, please, come to my house; we have a warm fire burning and you can get warm there. It's not far, and your bundle won't be too heavy."

Sitti felt it would be impolite to refuse, and besides, she was curious to see the people who dressed their cat in such elegant clothes. So Sitti and the kitten walked on through the olive orchard and onto the hillside beyond.

"You don't live in the village," Sitti said, surprised, since most people lived within village walls.

"No, we live in a cave in the hill," the little kitten replied.

And sure enough, in just a moment the kitten was knocking on a wooden door across the mouth of a cave. Sitti put her sticks and twigs down on the ground outside the door and straightened up to find that the door had been opened to them by another cat. This cat had a brown face and was wearing a blue dress and had a blue ribbon in her hair.

"So there you are, Leila," the cat said. "We have been worried sick about you. Come in, come in, Sitti, and get warm."

Sitti was overwhelmed by the sight that greeted her in the cave. The room was warm, even hot from the heat of an open fire, and all around the blaze, sitting comfortably on cushions, were cats of every size and color, dressed in every hue of the rainbow. There were cats in green and gold, in pink and red, in purple and lavender. Sitting nearest the fire was the largest and most beautiful cat Sitti had ever seen, dressed in white and wearing on her elegant black head a diamond crown. The cats helped Sitti sit down on a cushion, and they brought her a steaming hot glass of tea and some sesame cakes.

While Sitti ate and drank and grew warmer
and warmer, the cats talked and sang around
her. They were just like the people in the
village, Sitti realized. Some were gossiping,
some were telling stories, and some were
talking about politics. Soon Sitti found herself
talking with the cats around her about Im Yusuf.
"She's a very nice person, really," Sitti told the little
white cat dressed in blue who was sitting next to her.

14

"Isn't her son, Yusuf, the man who wants the mayor to extend the village walls?" asked the white cat.

While Sitti explained the village's need for more room, she ate her sesame cakes and drank her hot tea. She felt warmer and more comfortable than she had all winter and was very grateful to the cats for being kind to her. At last Sitti realized with a start that the time was getting late and she must leave if she were to get home before dark.

"This has been so very pleasant," Sitti said to the white cat, "but I really must leave because it is getting dark. Thank you so much for the lovely tea and cakes. You have been very kind to me, and I appreciate it."

"You are welcome, Sitti," the cat answered with a smile. "But before you leave, you must speak with our queen, Malika."

When Sitti reached the beautiful cat queen in her white dress, she bowed to her and said, "Thank you, Queen Malika, for your hospitality."

"We are the ones who should be thanking you, Sitti, for saving our naughty Leila," Queen Malika responded. "You are a good woman to consider the needs of a cat, and for your goodness I want to give you these two bags. One is full of onion peels and the other is full of garlic peels. Please take them with our thanks and put them under your bed tonight."

SESAME seeds are used to flavor a good number of Arabic foods. Small cakes or cookies are often topped with sesame seeds. "Simsim" is the Arabic word for sesame.

In Palestine, hot tea is drunk from small glasses much like juice glasses. Tea is called "Shy" in Arabic.

15

Sitti was too polite to comment on the strange gift, so she thanked the queen for the bags, and she left.

It was hard to carry the two bags of onion and garlic peels along with her bundle of twigs and sticks, but Sitti knew that if she left the bags behind the cats would know she didn't think much of their present. She couldn't leave the twigs and sticks behind because she really needed them. So she struggled home as best she could. It was a long walk, and it began to rain before she got to her house. Once or twice she stumbled on the way, and her back began to ache. But at last she made it home, put the bags down, and began a fire in her little brazier.

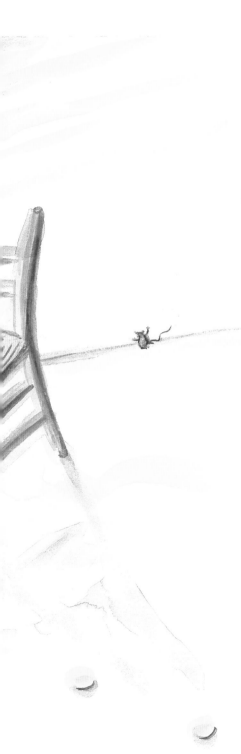

That night Sitti was too tired to eat, but she did remember to put the bags of onion and garlic peels under her bed. Sitti fell asleep the moment her head hit the pillow. Her sleep was filled with wonderful dreams of being warm and having lots of good things to eat.

The next morning dawned cold but bright, and Sitti lighted her little brazier to warm her house and heat her tea. She began to straighten up by folding her bedding and storing it away. When she saw the two bags the cats had given her, Sitti smiled and stooped down to pick them up and throw them away. Imagine her surprise when the bags that had been so light the night before were heavy and clunked when she lifted them. When Sitti opened the bags, she discovered they were filled with coins. In the night, the onion peels had turned into gold coins, and the garlic peels had turned into silver. Sitti could hardly believe her eyes. The cats' magic meant she could lead an easy life.

"I know just what I shall do first," Sitti said to herself as she took up a few coins of silver. "I'll buy Ali and his wife a few chickens so they can have their own eggs fresh every day."

Sitti's first thought when she discovered her good fortune was to think of the needs of her friends who had helped her when she was not so fortunate. So Sitti dressed and took some of her silver coins with her to buy gifts for her neighbors. She bought chickens for Ali, toys for the children of the olive orchard owner, and Turkish delight for Im Yusuf who had everything she really needed. Finally, Sitti bought a huge bundle of charcoal so she could keep herself warm.

Sitti's neighbors were surprised and pleased with the presents she gave them. Only Im Yusuf demanded to know where Sitti had found the money to buy such luxuries. And Sitti, because she could think of no reason not to, told Im Yusuf the story of the cats. But Im Yusuf, I'm sorry to tell you, was a selfish woman who thought only of herself; perhaps that is why she had such a sharp tongue and always found something unpleasant to say about others. When Sitti finished her tale, Im Yusuf immediately put on her shawl and boots and walked through the olive orchard and onto the hillside beyond. She strode up to the door of the cave and knocked loudly. When a cat dressed in lavender opened the door, Im Yusuf pushed her aside and walked in.

"Show me to your queen," she demanded rudely.

As soon as she saw the cat dressed in white, Im Yusuf continued. "Queen of the cats, you who call yourself Malika, I demand that you give me a bag of garlic peels and a bag of onion peels, just as you gave my neighbor, Sitti."

The bags were brought to Im Yusuf, who grabbed them and opened each one to make sure that they were full. Then she turned on her heel and left the cave without even saying thank you. Im Yusuf, you see, was not only selfish, she was also impolite. When she got home, Im Yusuf put the bags on the floor and put her bedding on top of them. Then she closed the shutters on her windows and locked them, and she locked her door so no one could steal the gold and silver coins she intended to get.

That night while Im Yusuf was asleep, the onion peels turned to wasps and the garlic peels turned to bees, and they buzzed around her, stinging her over and over again. Poor Im Yusuf yelled out, "Help, help," but no one could hear her because her shutters were closed and her door was locked. Finally, Sitti awoke and felt that something was wrong. She opened her door and thought she heard noises coming from Im Yusuf's house, so she walked over and knocked on Im Yusuf's door. When she heard the faint cry of "Help, help," Sitti took her ax and chopped down the door and rushed in. The bees and wasps flew out the open door, and Sitti was able to help Im Yusuf wash and put a soothing lotion on her stings.

You see, the magic of the cats was that the onion and garlic peels would become whatever the person they were given to deserved.

Sitti's goodness and kindness
caused the onion and garlic peels to become
coins, which the cats knew she
would use not only to help herself but to make others
happy too. Im Yusuf's greed and rudeness caused the
onion and garlic peels to become wasps and bees so
that Im Yusuf could feel the pain and hurt that she caused
others by her rudeness and her sharp tongue.

"Oh, Sitti," Im Yusuf cried, "I was so very wrong to try to
get gold and silver from the cats. I only wanted it to give to
my daughter-in-law because I thought she would
take me in if I gave her money."
"You know your daughter-in-law would take you in for
no money at all, Im Yusuf, if you would just be pleasant to
her," Sitti said as she tried to comfort Im Yusuf. "If you
really want some gold and silver, though, I'll give you some
of mine. I have more than enough to keep me warm and
happy for the rest of my life, and that is all
I really need from money."

I'm happy to say Im Yusuf learned from her mistake and became a much more pleasant person. She smiled more often and didn't say things to people to hurt their feelings. Her daughter-in-law was so pleased by Im Yusuf's new behavior that she invited her to live with them. Sitti still insisted on sharing her wealth, which she had gotten through kindness, with Im Yusuf, and they both lived happily until their deaths many years later. They told this story of their lives to all the children of the village, and they told the story to their children, so that when I was a little girl in the village, I, too, heard the story. I used to walk through the olive orchard looking up into the trees in hopes of seeing a little kitten dressed in lavender. But I never did, and now that I am older I know that the kitten only appears to those who really need warmth or food or love, and I always had plenty of those.

23

New Words
for
Young Readers

Tata (TAA Ta)   is another Arabic word for "Grandmother."

Jiddi (Jid Di)   means "Grandfather."

Jasmine   is a wonderful vine which grows in Palestine. It produces a small white blossom which is aromatic. Most of the old houses have jasmine (pronounced "yasmeen" in Arabic) growing over the doorway or windows. Yasmeen is another favorite name for a girl in Arabic.

Turkish delight   melts in your mouth. It is a very sweet candy that usually contains pistachio nuts and is dusted with powdered sugar.

Pistachio nuts   grow on trees around Aleppo, Syria and are called "Fustu Halabi" which is roughly translated into "Aleppo nuts."

Arabic bread   round loaves of flat bread which are called "pita" in America. These loaves of bread are used to scoop up food like a spoon, so that you eat the food and the bread simultaneously. A village like Shafa' Amer would always have a village oven. Women like Sitti would make their bread at home, let it rise, and then placing the bread on a round straw tray, the women would balance the tray on their heads and walk to the village oven. The village oven was my favorite place because I would play with other children there while our mothers talked and our bread baked. I would walk home eating a hot aromatic loaf of bread usually spread with a combination of spices called "zaater" which included sesame seeds.